A LORIMER BLUE KITE ADVENTURE

A Horse for Josie Moon

Sharon Siamon

James Lorimer & Company, Publishers
Toronto 1988

To Sylvia Braithwaite

1-55028-129-1 paper   1-55028-131-3 cloth

Illustrations: Elaine Macpherson

Canadian Cataloguing in Publication Data

Siamon, Sharon.
   A horse for Josie Moon

(A Lorimer blue kite adventure)
ISBN 1-55028-131-3 (bound)
ISBN 1-55028-129-1 (pbk.)

I. Title. II. Series.
PS8587.I225H67 1988   jC813'.54   C88-094853-1

James Lorimer & Company, Publishers
Egerton Ryerson Memorial Building
35 Britain Street
Toronto, M5A 1R7

Contents

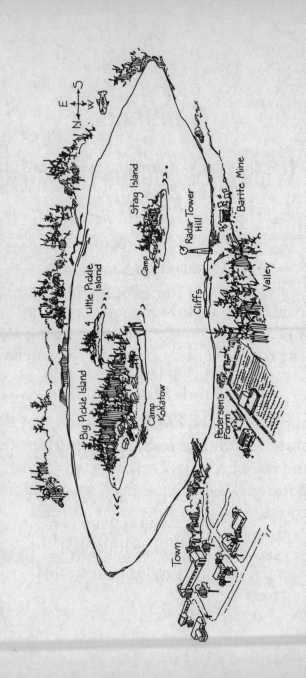

One

What's the Matter with Josie Moon?

Josie Moon came screaming over the waves in her powerboat, pretending she was riding her black stallion, Panther.

She twisted the wheel as if it were reins, and gave Panther an imaginary nudge with her knees. She could feel his muscles bunch under her as they bucked and dived. Of course the water wasn't water; it was lush fields of long golden grass. The ground thundered under Panther's pounding hooves.

Josie was eleven, going into grade six. Last year, in school, they'd watched a

film about a great black stallion. Since that day, Josie had been desperate for a horse — a horse of her own.

"Go, boy!" Josie shouted, and did a swift turn to the right. She and Panther swung round the corner of a hill. They lunged down the hill at top speed, reckless, wild and free.

At the same moment, a wood rowboat poked out from behind the rocks at the end of Big Pickle Island. Kiff Kokatow had been fishing for pickerel among the rocks, dragging his rubber worm over the lily pads, waiting for the torpedo-nosed fish to lunge for the bait.

Kiff was concentrating hard on his fishing, as usual. He didn't hear the roar of the approaching boat until the last second.

He looked up and saw a flash of green. Then he glimpsed Josie's face, frozen in terror at the wheel. Her boat, the *Green Hornet*, was heading straight for him.

Kiff dived over the side. The force of his dive kicked the old rowboat backwards. The *Green Hornet* brushed by, missing it by a hair.

"Josephine Moon! Are you for *real*?" Kiff bellowed, as the *Green Hornet* slowed, turned, and grumbled slowly back towards him.

Josie's face looked almost as green as her boat. She had missed smashing into Kiff by millimetres.

"Okay, Moonland, what's with the crazy driving?" Kiff shouted, swimming over to his boat. "What are you trying to do — kill somebody?"

"I didn't see you," Josie said in a low voice. She would never tell Kiff that she didn't see him because she was riding Panther across a golden plain. Wanting a horse was her secret.

"You were driving like a maniac," Kiff puffed, trying to haul his skinny, eleven-year-old body over the side of the boat. "I think your *parents* would be interested to know how close you came to cutting Camp Kokatow property in half...not to mention me!" Kiff lived at a fishing camp on Big Pickle Island. Camp Kokatow's wooden fishing boats were famous up and down the lake.

"Don't tell!" Josie said. "This summer is the first time they've let me take the *Green Hornet* out by myself. They'll never let me do it again, if you tell. I'll be grounded..."

"Dry ground — that's where you belong if you're going to drive like that!" Kiff had finally wriggled into the boat, and was wringing out the corners of his shirt.

He stared at Josie with curious brown eyes. He couldn't remember the last time Josie Moon had done something bad. She was usually perfect. Perfect in school, perfect at home, and sickeningly good in between. "What's the matter, Josie?" he said. "Did you forget to take your perfect person pill this morning?"

"Just don't tell," Josie said. Her dark eyes were full of worry.

"I might be persuaded not to tell…" Kiff said slowly. He was enjoying this moment. Usually, he was the one in deep trouble. Usually, *he* was begging for mercy.

"If…?" Josie asked.

"If you let me drive the *Green Hornet*," Kiff said in one quick breath. The *Hornet* was the fastest boat on the lake. He'd been wanting to drive it as long as he could remember.

"What?" Josie screeched.

"You heard me. *I vant to drive your boat!*" Kiff gave her a Dracula grin.

"I can't do that!" Josie shouted. "My parents would kill me if I lent the boat to someone else!" The *Hornet's* motor was still idling, and she had to resist the temptation to gun it and get away from Kiff and his maddening grin.

"Me and Odie," Kiff said. "We *both* want a nice long drive." Odie was Kiff's best friend. He lived on the mainland, near the town of Big Pickle Lake.

Josie yanked the elastics on her ponytails tight. "I'll think about it," she said stiffly.

"Don't think too long, Spaceface! Otherwise I'll have to tell, in great detail, how you came flying across the lake like a rocket...."

"All right!" Josie couldn't stand any more. "You can drive the *Green Hornet*...someday." She pushed hard on the throttle and the *Hornet's* engine burst into full roar.

"Soon!" Kiff shouted as the *Green Hornet* shot away. He watched it swoop out of sight around the end of the island. "Nice boat," he grinned wickedly. "I wonder what's going on with old Josie Moon?"

Two

Little Pickle Island

Panther seemed a bit jittery as Josie brought him up to his home dock. "Easy, boy," she said, pulling back on the throttle. No wonder Panther was upset! Almost crashing into Kiff Kokatow would make anyone nervous, Josie thought.

She tied Panther's reins to a metal ring on the dock and jumped ashore. As she made sure the rope was tight, Josie's big black horse became just a green motorboat again. A motorboat she had promised to lend to Kiff!

There's no way I can do it, Josie thought. If my parents ever found out....

The *Green Hornet* wasn't just a high-powered toy. Josie's parents worked for the Wildlife Service. Sometimes they got emergency calls and had to get from their island to the mainland in a hurry.

Josie firmly pushed Kiff and her problem to the back of her mind. She had to think about how to get her horse. She looked around the tiny chunk of rock her family called home. "If only Little Pickle Island weren't *so* little!" she sighed out loud.

There was just room on the island for the Moon's small white house and a boathouse. At one time there had been a little barn, but that had been torn down. Now a scrappy patch of blueberries grew where the barn used to stand, and one pine tree rose out of a crack in the rock.

Until she'd started wanting a horse, Josie had loved her island. It lay curled behind Big Pickle Island like a dill pickle next to a bigger dill pickle in a jar. It had always been her own private world. But now, suddenly, she seemed to have outgrown that world. There was no place here for a horse to run, and a horse couldn't graze on solid rock!

Feeling impatient, Josie strode up the dock and pushed open the little door of the boathouse. The light was dim inside, and it smelled of wood and gas and lake water. If only this boathouse were a barn, Josie thought, with a warm stall in the middle instead of a cold square of black water....

Actually, Josie thought, there *would* be room for a stall, if only this boathouse weren't so crammed with junk! She started shifting things around. She moved the gas cans, canoe paddles, and odds and ends of lumber to the far side of the boathouse.

There! Now you could see where a stall might go. Josie could almost see Panther standing there, shiny black where the rays of light from the small window touched his back.

At that moment the big front doors swung open, letting in a blaze of sunlight.

Josie jumped. "Oh! Hi, Mom."

"Josie! I heard the boat come back, and I wondered where you'd got to." Caroline Moon shielded her eyes with her hands to see Josie better. "What are you doing?"

"Just cleaning up. Doesn't it look great?"

Her mother frowned. "It looks amazing — but where's my spare gas can?"

Josie dug her mother's gas can out of the heap on the boathouse floor. "We *could* fit a horse stall in here," she said.

"Horse? Josie, you're not still dreaming about getting a horse, are you?" Her mother shook her head. "We've talked that all through...." Her blue eyes were warm with sympathy as she gazed at her daughter standing rigidly still, the gas can in her hand. "It's no use, Josie. You know you can't have a horse on the island."

Caroline Moon buckled on her life jacket and tossed another to Josie. "I'm going to town," she said. "Want to come?"

Josie thought for a second. "Sure," she said. "I wouldn't mind going over to Odie's farm."

Josie's mother looked surprised. "I didn't know you and Odie Pedersen were friends."

"We're *not*." Josie climbed into the boat. "But I want to look around. Odie's grandfather used to have horses."

"Josephine Moon!" Her mother shook her blonde, curly head. "It's got to stop. You can have a goat, or a parrot, or a pet armadillo on Little Pickle Island, but you can never have a horse. If a horse fell out of the sky into this boat right now, you couldn't keep it." She slammed the boathouse door. *"Just quit talking about a horse!"*

Josie followed her mother into the boat, and glanced up at the clear summer sky as they backed out into the lake.

If a horse fell out of the sky, she thought, I might call him Skydive instead of Panther. Josie Moon did not give up easily.

Three

The *Green Hornet*

"We're going to drop in at Camp Kokatow on our way," shouted Josie's mother over the roar of the *Green Hornet*'s motor.

"Do we have to?" Josie bellowed back. The last person in the world she wanted to see was Kiff Kokatow!

"Yes, we have to. I want to see if Sheila needs anything in town." Sheila was Kiff's mother. "What's the matter with you, Josie?"

Josie just shook her head. Maybe they wouldn't even see Kiff. Maybe he'd be hauling garbage, or scrubbing out-houses. She hoped so.

But as the *Green Hornet* surged up to the Camp Kokatow dock Josie could see Kiff and his mother waving a greeting. The camp was quiet. At dawn, all the guests had gone out fishing in the Camp Kokatow boats. By dusk, they'd all be back, bragging, bustling around the dock and cleaning their fish.

"You're just the person I want to see, Josie." Sheila Kokatow smiled as she reached for the *Green Hornet*'s bow. Kiff was too busy eating a sandwich to help them dock, Josie noticed. "I need lots of blueberries for pies, if you have any time for picking. I'm paying fifty cents a container." Sheila made hundreds of blueberry pies each summer for the Camp Kokatow guests.

"Sure!" Josie nodded. Fifty cents a container would come in handy. There were lots of expenses with a horse — hay, a saddle, reins, horseshoes....

"I stopped by to see if there's anything you need in town," Caroline Moon said.

"More bananas," Kiff mumbled through his sandwich. "I'm eating the last one."

"You eat more than all my paying guests combined!" Sheila Kokatow laughed, ruffling Kiff's untidy brown head.

He looked embarrassed. "Is it my fault I'm addicted to banana and marshmallow sandwiches?"

"Is that what you're eating?" Josie blurted. She couldn't believe some of the things Kiff ate.

Kiff just grinned. He swept the *Green Hornet* with greedy eyes. "Nice boat you have there," he said. "It sure must be fun to drive."

"Would you like to ride over to town with us?" Caroline Moon asked. "We'll be coming back in about an hour."

NO! Josie screeched inwardly.

"I'd love to." Kiff flashed his maddening grin at Josie. "I can go visit Odie."

Josie was seething inside as they pulled away from the dock. Why did her mother have to ask *him*? Josie knew she could forget going to Pedersen's farm now! Odie and Kiff would follow her around until they found out what she was doing there. Then Kiff would tease her about wanting a horse until she broke out in a rash!

Kiff swallowed the last bite of his disgusting sandwich. "I saw Josie driving the *Green Hornet* all by herself today," he hollered over the noise of the motor. "Looked like a lot of fun...."

Josie froze. What was he going to say?

"Well, Josie has a lot of experience and she's a very careful driver," Mrs. Moon shouted back. "Her father and I trust her."

Kiff shrugged and shot a meaningful glance at Josie.

"Where is Dad?" Josie roared, hoping to change the subject.

"He had to go post some notices in campgrounds," said Caroline Moon. "They're not allowing any open fires until we get a good rain. There's a big forest fire burning a couple of hundred kilometres north of here."

"So I guess he'll be gone all day." Kiff fired another look at Josie.

NO! Josie screamed inwardly again. You can't drive our boat today! She glared at Kiff, hating his smug smile, his mocking brown eyes, his ugly, turned-up nose. Why did he have to be the only other kid who lived on the islands? Why did their parents have to be such good friends? Why was she stuck with him day after day, year after year, summer after summer. It wasn't fair! As soon as she had Panther she could ride away from Kiff Kokatow, free as the wind. In the meantime...

"Josie said she was going to Odie's too." Caroline Moon's voice broke into Josie's thoughts.

"Mo-ther!" Josie moaned under her breath. "Did you have to tell him?" She had to stop her mother from saying any more. They were at the town dock, and Kiff jumped ashore to tie up. He was looking at Josie with a curious frown.

"Yes, I — uh — thought I'd do some collecting...at Odie's farm," Josie stammered. It was true, in a way. She'd be collecting information about horses. But she'd have to think up a story to satisfy Kiff, and fast!

"Well, have a good time, you two, but be back here to meet me in an hour," Caroline Moon said. She set off up the dock towards the main street of town.

"*Now* would be a good time for that little boat trip we were talking about," Kiff said, when she'd gone. "Your dad's away all day, your mom's shopping...."

"NO!" Josie wanted to pound him. "There are too many people around. You heard my mom. She trusts me."

"Well, she wouldn't if I told her that you almost swamped my boat today. I'm not going to wait forever. Just keep that in mind." Kiff turned and began walking up the long town dock. Then he stopped and looked at her. "What are you collecting at Odie's farm?" he asked.

Josie walked slowly after him. She didn't answer Kiff's question till they turned left on the road that led along the lakeshore to Odie Pedersen's farm. "Mushrooms," she said.

Four

Deadly Mushrooms?

"Mushrooms are dangerous," Kiff said. "They can be deadly poisonous."

"That's why I'm collecting them," Josie said. "In case I want to poison somebody."

Kiff walked on silently for a moment. "But why would you look for mushrooms on Odie's farm?" he asked. "I've never seen any mushrooms there."

"That's because you don't know where to look!" Josie shot back. "There used to be horses on Pedersen's farm, right?"

"Sure. Odie's grandfather had them for pulling logs out of the bush."

"And horses make manure, right?" Josie went on.

Kiff wrinkled his nose. "I'll say. There's a pile as high as a pyramid behind the barn. What does that have to do with mushrooms?"

"Mushrooms," said Josie matter-of-factly, "grow in manure."

"You mean the mushrooms we eat?" Kiff made a gagging noise.

"Of course," Josie said. "You know that black stuff that's always stuck to them...?"

"Josie Moon, YOU'RE WEIRD!" Kiff shouted. He took off down the path towards Odie's farm.

Josie stared after him. Look who's calling *me* weird! she thought. Kiff Kokatow used to carry live worms in his pockets. Back in grade three he made meatloaf out of moose meat, spiced it up with fly dope, and brought it to a school lunch! Now he eats marshmallow and banana sandwiches. Yuck! I could never be as weird as Kiff if I lived to be a hundred. Kiff Kokatow is the wizard of weird!

It didn't matter what Kiff called her anyway. Now she could poke around Odie's barn and not worry about those two nosing in. Kiff was afraid of a bit of horse manure and a few poisoned mushrooms!

As she walked up the lane, she could see Odie and Kiff on the wide front porch of Odie's place. Josie liked the Pedersen's farm. The house and barn were made like the farms back in Sweden, where Odie's grandparents had come from. The grassy fields stretched right down to the water's edge. It was, Josie thought, a perfect place for a horse.

"Here comes the Hyper-space Mushroom Monster," Kiff snorted, poking Odie in the ribs. "What she cooks, you'd better not eat!"

"Or drink!" Josie shot back. "I can make a poisoned mushroom drink that will drop you dead in twelve hours. And there's no antidote!"

Odie's straight blond hair was sticking up the way it always did when he didn't plaster it down with water. Josie liked Odie a lot better when he wasn't with Kiff. Then he could actually be semi-human.

"Is that true, Josie?" Odie asked curiously. "Could you really drop us dead?"

"Of course," Josie said. "If I found some *Amanita phalloides*, or death cap, as they call it." She launched into a long scientific explanation of the different kinds of deadly mushrooms. It was the kind of stuff you knew about when your parents' work was studying plants.

"Boring, boring, boring," Kiff groaned at last. "Go find your old mushrooms. Odie and I have more interesting things to talk about — such as boat trips...."

Josie ignored him. "I'm just going to look around behind your barn," she said to Odie.

"Go ahead," Odie shrugged. "My Granddad's back there."

Josie turned her back on the two boys and strolled away, remembering to examine the ground as if she were hunting for mushrooms.

It was really the inside of the old barn she wanted to see. Olaf Pedersen, Odie's grandfather, was cutting the long grass behind the barn with a huge curved knife. Josie watched while he cut handfuls of the grass, twisted them together, and stacked them in a small, neat pyramid.

He stopped when he saw Josie watching him, and mopped his forehead with a handkerchief. "That's an old country way to stack hay," he explained. "We used to grow lots of hay for the horses." He shook his head. "Got no horses now, but I still do it — just to keep my hands busy, I guess. I hate to see good hay go to waste."

Josie felt a tingle. It wouldn't go to waste when she got Skydive! "How many horses did you have on the farm?" she asked.

"We had two teams. There was Kate and Nellie, and Betsy and Dagmar. Ah! they were good beasts. Do you know? All their harness is still over there in the barn." The old man laughed. "I just never could throw it away."

Josie's excitement spread down to her toes. "That harness must be pretty old," she said. "You probably couldn't use it any more. And I guess you didn't have saddles and bridles and stuff for riding horses."

"Sure, we have some — and it's not that old," he laughed again. "Anyhow, I clean it up every so often. I guess the old days are never going to come back — but we can't waste good leather."

"Are there still any horses around Big Pickle Lake?"

"Not many around anymore," the old man mused. "In the old days, every lumber camp and mine had horses. When those mines and camps closed up, everybody just left on the next train, left everything behind — even dishes on the table and pots on the stove. Sometimes they left the horses too. Some of them, or their children or grandchildren, might still be running wild in the bush. I don't know, young Josie. That would be thirty, forty years ago and more." Olaf shook his head.

"Could I see the old tack?" Josie asked, a little breathlessly.

"Oh, sure." Olaf Pedersen smiled. "You go take a look. Don't bump your head on the manure scoop, now."

Quickly Josie ran to the barn and slipped in through an open door. She had never been in Odie's barn before. It was dusty and dim. There was a track running along the low ceiling, with a metal bucket like the front end of a bulldozer hanging from it. That must be the scoop Olaf was talking about, Josie thought. I wonder how it worked?

She gave the scoop a shove, and to her surprise it shot along the track, flew

out the open door and flipped — right over the old manure pile. Mr. Pedersen must keep this running too, even though there isn't any more manure to shovel, Josie thought. She stepped out to pull the scoop back in. She gave it another shove and it glided along to the end of the row of stalls.

The horse stalls had high walls and metal rings for tying the horses. The barn had a warm smell, like old wood and ripe grass. Josie could almost hear the stamp of horses' hooves, and the echo of soft whinnying from long ago.

She walked past the row of stalls and into a smaller room at the front of the barn.

This was a treasure house! The room was filled with old leather tack, hung on wooden pegs on the walls. There were reins and horse collars, and bridles, and even a saddle. The leather had a special smell all its own. Josie reached out to feel a set of reins. They were cobwebby and dusty, but still soft.

Mr. Pedersen was right! He'd kept it all in good condition. When I get Skydive or Panther, Josie thought happily, I can probably borrow…

"Any mushrooms in there?" came a sudden muffled laugh. Josie spun around in time to see two heads disappear into the old manure scoop.

She walked quickly and silently towards the scoop. They had been watching her! A spike of Odie's hair appeared above the edge. Josie reached up and gave the scoop a mighty shove.

The manure scoop went flying down the ceiling track. It went even faster when properly loaded, Josie was happy to see.

"HEY! WHO? Odie, what's happening?" That was Kiff.

"Oh, no! Josie, what have you done? Look out!" Odie roared.

"Hold on!"

"Ahhh!"

There was a satisfying plop as the scoop dumped both boys onto the top of the manure pile. "Right where you belong!" Josie called as she ducked out the front door of the barn. "I hope you choke on a mushroom."

"Moonbrain, you're dead!" she could hear Kiff hollering behind her. "Wait till I catch up with you!"

No chance! She'd be safely back at the town dock to meet her mother before Kiff managed to dust himself off.

Five

Blood On The Saddle

Going back in the boat Josie sat in the middle of the *Green Hornet*, between Kiff and her mother. She hoped this would keep Kiff from talking, but it didn't work. He just had to shout louder.

"So — uh — where does Josie keep her poison mushroom collection?" he boomed. "In the fridge?"

"Poison mushrooms?" Caroline Moon looked puzzled.

"Oops. Sorry. Maybe you didn't know Josie was collecting fatal fungi."

Oh, sure! You're very sorry, Josie thought. You have the biggest mouth in the universe, Kiff Kokatow!

"Josie has a lot of new ideas this summer," Mrs. Moon grinned. "I knew about the horses, but I hadn't heard anything about mushrooms."

"Horses?" Kiff's eyes ballooned with curiosity.

MOM! Josie wanted to shriek, but it was too late.

"Didn't Josie tell you?" Mrs. Moon laughed. "She's determined to have a horse on our tiny island. I thought she was doing some horse research today at Odie's."

"Well now, maybe she was." Kiff flashed a big grin at Josie. "But she told Odie and me she was looking for mushrooms." In a lower voice that only Josie could hear he said, "So old Josie Moon is horse crazy. Just wait till I tell Odie!"

Josie wanted to drown him.

Josie's mother jumped out of the boat at Camp Kokatow to take a package and a message to Sheila Kokatow. But Kiff hung around the dock.

"I know a good song about a horse," Kiff said. "Want to hear it?"

"No," Josie said.

"I think I'll sing it anyway. It's one of my favourite songs." Kiff threw back his shoulders, aimed his voice out over the lake, and roared out:

> There was blood on the saddle,
> And blood on the ground,
> And a great big puddle,
> Of blood all around.

"Kiff, that's disgusting. Stop that."

> The cowgirl lay in it,
> All covered with gore,
> And she won't go riding,
> Her bronco no more.

Josie stuck her fingers in her ears. "I'm not listening, so you might as well stop."

"Just one more verse, Moonface, and this is the best," said Kiff.

O pity poor Josie,
All bloody and red,
For her bronco fell on her,
And mashed in her head.

Kiff finally stopped singing. "A bronco — that's a kind of horse, eh, Josie?" he said. "I'm not surprised you want a bronco. You already have a face like a horse."

Josie leaped out of the *Green Hornet*, leaving it rocking wildly, and raced after Kiff up the dock. Kiff couldn't usually outrun Josie, but he had a head start.

"You could ask for a horse for your birthday..." he sang out over his shoulder as he reached the path leading up the hill to the Camp Kokatow cabins.

Josie chased him up the path.

"Or enter a Win a Horse contest," Kiff shouted, as he ducked around the corner of the nearest cabin.

Josie went around the cabin the other way.

"Or get your rich uncle to send you one from California," he laughed as Josie grabbed him by both arms.

"I don't have a rich uncle, and in a minute you're not going to have a face!" Josie panted.

"Well, eat lots of cereal and send in box tops. They'll send you a horse," Kiff shot back. "About two centimetres tall."

"Quit talking about my horse!" Josie shouted.

"You know," Kiff went on, "one of those plastic horses about as big as your nose."

Josie let go of Kiff to punch him in the nose, but he twisted out from under her arm.

"It's going to have to be a mighty small horse to fit on Little Pickle Island."

Kiff would tease her all summer, Josie thought furiously. He was one of those people who never got sick of teasing, never stopped thinking up new ways to torture you. The only way to make him quit was to stop caring about whatever he was teasing you about. It had always worked in the past. She dropped her hands and shrugged. "You're a slimeball,

Kokatow," she said, and turned her back on him.

But Josie knew she couldn't stop caring about horses. Underneath her anger was a great secret excitement. Her visit to Odie's farm — seeing the tack room and hearing Olaf Pedersen's stories about the wild horses that might still roam the bush — had just made it worse. If those stories are true, Dad will know, Josie thought.

Six

The Wild Horses of Ramore

The forest fire danger kept Josie's father at work until almost dark.

At last Josie heard the purr of the twenty-five horsepower motor that drove their old steel boat. It was green, like the *Green Hornet*, big and rugged enough to go anywhere. She heard the boat long before she saw it cruise out of the shadow of Big Pickle Island toward the dock.

"Hello, Jo," her dad smiled, as she bent down to catch the boat's bow. Bill Moon had straight dark hair, like Josie's, and the same thoughtful brown eyes. He had been born on a Cree Reserve near Big Pickle Lake. He felt as at home in a boat as he did on land.

Josie helped him tie the bow and stern securely to the dock. "I was waiting for you," she said. "I wanted to ask you something."

"Can it wait until I've had my dinner?" Bill asked. "It's been a long day."

"I guess so," Josie said. "It's about horses."

"Oh, then I'm sure it *can't* wait," her father chuckled. "Anything about horses is a matter of life and death!"

"Dad, don't joke," Josie pleaded. "Do you know, did you ever hear of any wild horses around here? Odie's grandfather said some got left behind when the mines closed down, and they might still be running wild."

Her father collected his gear from the boat and headed towards the house. "Well, not around here," he said at last. "But there's supposed to be a small herd of feral horses up around Ramore. It's not my area, so I don't really know too much about them."

"What's 'feral' mean?" Josie kept up to her father's long strides.

"Wild." Bill Moon said. "A feral horse is one that's gone back to the wild. It's a wild animal, just the same as a moose or wolf. This herd would be the descendants of the original horses. They'd be just as shy of humans as any wild animal — and just about as hard to tame."

"But how do they live, without people?" Josie asked. "How do they get through the winter?'

"Oh, they grow a big thick, shaggy coat, and they paw through the snow to get at the dry grass. Horses are pretty tough."

"I know," Josie said. "Horses are terrific."

Bill paused outside the lighted windows of the Moon's front porch. "You know I'd be glad to let you keep a horse — if we lived somewhere else," he said.

"You *would*?" Josie felt her heart leap with excitement.

"But," her father went on, "we live on Little Pickle Island." He gestured around the tiny bubble of rock. "A good place for people, but not for horses." He opened the screen door. "I smell food," he breathed deeply. "Don't stay out too much longer Josie. It's getting dark."

"I won't," Josie promised, and went to sit by the edge of the water and let her thoughts flow around her. The Wild Horses of Ramore! They would be proud and free, Josie thought, just as she imagined her black stallion would be.

She could picture him so clearly. She could imagine brushing his long mane, and feeding him, and riding…. Suddenly the memory of her wild ride in the *Green Hornet* flooded back.

That's how it would feel to ride a horse, Josie thought. As if you had all the power in the universe at your command. It had been fantastic!

Suddenly the memory of Kiff's boat looming in front of her swept over Josie. How could she have driven the *Hornet* like some dumb demolition derby driver? Never in her life had she done anything so stupid! The worst part of it was, she wasn't sure she wouldn't do it again!

****

Josie dreamed that Kiff Kokatow was driving the *Green Hornet* towards a wall of rock. The motor roared as it sped straight at the cliff! She woke with a start and sat up in bed. She *did* hear the sound of the *Hornet's* motor, but it was fading. The *Hornet* was leaving the island!

Josie's mother was sitting at her desk as Josie ran into the kitchen. Caroline Moon had first come to Big Pickle Lake as a student on a summer project. Now she knew as much about the north and felt as comfortable in the woods as Josie's father. Her desk was under a corner window. Caroline Moon liked to wake up early and work with the morning sun streaming in.

"Who took the boat?" Josie blurted.

Her mother looked up, surprised. "Your dad had to go in early," she said. "There's a small fire burning northwest of here."

"Is it bad?" Josie asked. She knew how dangerous a forest fire could be this time of year.

"Not yet," Caroline Moon turned back to her work. "It seems to have started early this morning. They're going to try and stamp it out quickly. They've asked all the staff to be on call. I may have to go in later, too."

"That's all right," Josie said. Her nightmare fears of Kiff racing the *Green Hornet* finally faded in the clear summer light of the kitchen. It was a perfect day for picking blueberries, Josie thought. She would take her canoe along the shore and stop at the best berry patches. Then she'd paddle around to Camp Kokatow and collect fifty cents a container from Kiff's mother. It would all be "horse money."

Josie didn't bother her mother about breakfast. She knew where the cereal was, under the green-checked cloth that hung from the sink counter. It was in a sealed can, not a box. All of the Moons' food had to be in metal cans because of the mice and ants that shared the kitchen with them.

When Josie finished her cereal she took the waxed paper from the empty can and polished the warm top of the woodstove. The heavy paper made the black metal gleam. Then she stuffed the used paper into the stove to burn. They burned all their boxes and paper in the black iron woodstove. The Moons had to carry all their garbage to the dump on the mainland, so very little got thrown away.

Plastic containers got saved for things like picking blueberries. Josie found enough of them under the sink to cover the bottom of the canoe.

"I'm going berry-picking, Mom," Josie said, as she pumped water from a hand pump beside the sink to rinse out her cereal bowl.

"Good," her mother muttered, without looking up. "Don't paddle across the lake by yourself. The wind's supposed to come up later today."

"I won't," Josie said, but she wished her mother hadn't said that. The best blueberries were across the lake.

Outside, it was hard to believe a wind was coming. The island lay as still as a picture, reflected perfectly in the mirror of the lake.

"I see the *Hornet*'s gone," Josie heard a voice say. She whipped around to see Kiff balancing on one foot on top of a survey stake that had been pounded into the rock.

"Yes, and I'm glad!" Josie shifted her bag of containers angrily to her other shoulder. She could see Kiff's Camp Kokatow rowboat down at the dock.

"Did you row all the way over here just to bug me about a boat ride?"

"Sooner or later," Kiff grinned. "You *know* I'm going to drive that boat." He looked curiously at her. "What's in the bag? Mushrooms?"

"I'm going berry-picking, as if it were any of your business." She swung off towards the boathouse, where her green canoe was stored.

"Poison berries or ordinary ones?" Kiff asked.

"BLUEBERRIES! you twit. For your mother."

"I thought of going berry-picking myself," Kiff said, hopping down from his stake. He hadn't really thought about it, but he knew it would bug Josie if he went along. "I'll come with you," he said.

"You will not! Anyway, you don't have any containers." Josie looked at the bare bottom of Kiff's boat.

"I have the best container of all," Kiff said. "My mouth." He pointed at his open mouth. "Never spills, easy to carry around, and never gets full."

"Well, it's certainly *big* enough!" Josie said. "I don't care if you go picking or not, but you're not coming in my canoe. I haven't got room for dead weight."

"I'll paddle...in the front," Kiff said quickly. He knew how Josie loved to steer. "You can go a lot faster with two paddlers." He gave Josie a wicked grin. "Or I could just stay here and chat with your mother," he shrugged. "About boats, and things."

Josie felt the promise of the day dim like a lantern sputtering on a dark night. "All right," she groaned. "But you only eat what *you* pick. I'm trying to make some money."

As they hoisted Josie's green canoe out of the boathouse and into the warm lake water, Josie had one brightening thought. Her mother had told her to stay close to shore in case of a strong wind. With Kokatow aboard, she could go anywhere. At least he was good for something — even if it was just weighing down the front of the canoe.

Seven

Radar Tower Hill

The slim green canoe slid away from the dock with hardly a ripple.

"Want to hear some more horse songs?" Kiff asked from the bow.

"No, and don't sing any if you want to stay in this canoe," Josie said.

"Blueberry songs?"

"No."

"Paddling songs? How about:

My paddle clean and bright,
Flashing like sil-ver,
Follow the wild goose flight,
Dip, dip and swing.

Kiff swung his paddle high in the air, showering Josie with water.

Josie swung the canoe around, heading back to shore. "I should have known better than to bring you along!"

"Okay, no more swinging the paddle or splashing," Kiff promised. "Let's go over to the Radar Tower Hill."

Josie stopped paddling. The abandoned radar station was across the lake, where the blueberries were best. The rocks rose steeply from the water to a high rock dome. On the very top was the old radar dish. It was on the highest point of land, and twenty years ago had been used to watch for unfriendly aircraft. Now it was out of date, and no one used it any more.

Josie had been thinking about exploring the old radar station for a long time. It was a wild piece of shoreline. There were no fishing camps or cottages on that part of the lake, and not many places to dock. But Josie knew a couple of spots where you could nose a canoe into a narrow notch in the rocks and tie it up safely. She headed the canoe across the lake.

Kiff was a good paddler when he quit kidding around. They were almost perfectly matched in skill and strength, so the canoe flew through the water.

In a few minutes they had reached the cliffs and tied up the canoe. There was just a narrow ledge to stand on along the base of the cliff, and a long hard climb ahead.

"There should be great blueberries up there," Josie squinted upwards. "They get lots of sun."

The cliffs faced the morning sun, and the rock under Josie's bare feet was already hot as they started to climb. The moss and lichen had dried in the heat to a crisp crackly carpet that tickled and prickled underfoot.

"Ouch!" Kiff complained. "I should have brought my shoes."

"You get a better grip barefoot," Josie panted. "Come on, Kokatow, don't be such a wimp." She clung to the roots of pines to pull herself up. The young pines grew in skimpy patches of soil, and sent their bare roots snaking down the cliff face in search of moisture. They were almost as good to climb as a ladder. And in the shady places, under the pine boughs, Josie found more blueberries than she had ever seen in one place.

Halfway up, they sat like eagles on a mountain ledge, with the smell of warm pine resin all around them, and the hot buzz of crickets filling the air. At first they just sat and panted and looked — down out over the blue blue lake, over Big Pickle Island and the lake beyond. Then down at the ground where a dark blue carpet of sun-warmed berries made it hard to move without squishing enough to fill a dish.

At last Josie grabbed a container out of her sack and began raking the berries into it.

Kiff sat and stuffed himself. "I'm not moving," he told Josie. "I'm never moving from this spot." The berries flew into his mouth.

"You're such a pig!" Josie said. "You could pick enough here for twenty pies for your mom."

"Why wait for pies?" Kiff asked. "Blueberries taste better like this anyway. My mom should just send the fishermen up here for dessert. They spend all day on the lake catching fish for dinner, why wouldn't they climb a cliff for dessert?"

Josie grinned. "You're so weird, Kiff Kokatow, you could probably talk them into it!" Kiff was famous around Big Pickle Lake for telling tall tales to fishermen from the city. There was something about his big round eyes and freckled face that made them believe almost anything he said.

Josie carefully put lids on her full containers and set them under the tree. "Touch those blueberries and you die. I'm going higher up. You stay here and stuff yourself."

"Don't worry," Kiff said. "Years from now, when you come back, rich and famous, I'll still be here, eating."

Josie worked her way higher up the cliff. The trees got thinner and smaller and the sun hotter as she neared the top. Under the radar dish's steel legs, even the blueberries were scorched by the sun. Nothing grew on the hot, bald rock.

Josie wished she'd worn a hat. She held up her hand to shield her eyes and stared out across the vista of lakes and trees to the east. She could see all of Big Pickle Lake now, stretching nearly ten kilometres north and south.

Far below her she could faintly hear Kiff singing.

> *Just plant a blueberry on my grave,*
> *And let the juice (slurp!) slip through!*

Josie turned and walked a few steps across the top of the bare ridge so she could see into the valley on the other side. This slope fell less steeply, and there was a clear path running down through the pines and poplars. Far off on the northwest horizon, Josie saw a pillar of grey smoke. The fire! She wondered if her father was there. She wondered if the fire was spreading!

Josie's head started to feel light from the brightness and heat. Maybe down the other side of the hill it would be cooler. At the bottom of the hill was a small clearing in the trees, and a grassy meadow.

Josie took a few steps down the path towards the meadow. She stopped in the cool shadow of a pine. It was so quiet on this side of the hill that she could hear the bees buzzing in the shade.

Suddenly Josie gave a start. It wasn't bees. Just to her right hung the biggest paper wasps' nest she'd ever seen. If she'd blundered into it, instead of moving slowly and calmly...! Josie had been stung by wasps, and it was the worst pain she could think of.

She edged very carefully out from under the tree, and sat on the path to catch her breath. So much for the shade!

It was hot. The sun bathed everything in a golden light. Josie saw something move at the edge of the clearing. She wasn't afraid of animals; she had often watched them from her canoe as they came down to the lake to drink.

Whatever she was watching was light brown, like a deer. It stood in the dappled shadows of the forest, so still that if Josie hadn't seen it move she wouldn't be able to make it out.

Then it moved again. Josie caught her breath. A horse came full into the clearing, tossed its head to shoo the flies, and began to eat.

Josie rubbed her eyes. It was sunstroke, for sure! I've been wishing for a horse so badly that now I'm seeing things! she thought. It can't be a horse, back here in the bush. I should have worn a hat!

Josie blinked again. A second horse stepped out of the woods to join the first. This one was chestnut-coloured, and taller. It flicked its tail and buried its head in the long grass.

Then a third horse came out of the trees, and finally a young horse. It was pale grey with a lighter mane and tail.

The young horse was more interested in playing than eating. It frisked around the grown-up horses, tossing its heels in the air, running up and down the slope and sniffing the wind in all directions.

Once, Josie thought the smaller horse spied her up on the hill. It made a few running steps in her direction, stopped, and whinnied.

The other horses lifted their heads as if to say, "What now?" The young horse tossed its head and whinnied again.

"Skydive!" Josie said out loud. "You're real, and you're here!"

Eight

Horses and Blueberries

Josie backed slowly and quietly up the hill. When she reached the top she slid and scrambled down to the ledge.

"Kiff!" she shouted, "KOKATOW! Come here and see!"

Kiff was still eating. "Come and see what?" he mumbled with his mouth full. "More blueberries? No thanks. I've got enough here to keep me busy."

"HORSES!" Josie panted. "There are horses on the other side of the hill. Come on!" She dragged Kiff to his feet.

"You're nuts," Kiff grumbled, "if you think I'm going to believe you saw horses on the other side of this hill."

They scrambled to the top of the hill and looked down the other side. The clearing was empty.

"There were four of them," Josie cried. "Right over there."

"Any elephants?" Kiff asked. "Giraffes, maybe?"

"Kiff, I'm not kidding. They were real. I saw them. Four horses. Three adults and a colt."

"You've really gone horse crazy, Josie Moon-a-roony," Kiff sighed. "Too bad. You were a nice kid, once."

"Kiff, stop that. They must have left tracks...." Josie started down the hill. "I can follow them."

In the valley, where Josie had seen the horses graze, there were no hoof prints. The ground was too dry, and the grass too thick and matted to leave a trace.

"They were here!" Josie cried in despair.

"Well, something was here," Kiff pointed to some trampled weeds. "Something big. Sure it wasn't elephants you saw?"

"Kiff!"

"Or maybe elk?" Kiff said, stopping his teasing for a second.

"Elk?"

"Elk are sort of like horses — big, white down the front. Or maybe it was Santa's reindeer!" Kiff couldn't resist.

Josie was shaking her head. "There was a young one, a horse about this high." Josie held up her hand. "He was grey, with a light mane."

"We'd better get you home. It must be the heat," Kiff said, starting back up the hill.

"Wait, Kiff, what's over here? Is there a farm or something back in the woods? An old homestead?"

"There's not much except the radar station for fifty kilometres on this side of the lake," Kiff said. "There's maybe an old prospector's shack or two and that abandoned barite mine down the shore, but nothing else. Just bush."

Josie nodded. She knew the barite mine. It was an old open-pit mine, abandoned for years. She had never been allowed to play around the pit or mine shacks because of the danger of cave-ins.

"Well, those horses had to come from somewhere," Josie said.

"From your imagination, that's where," Kiff told her. "I'm going back. If you don't hurry up I'll eat all the berries in your containers."

"You'd better not!"

"I might." Kiff started up the hill. "What do you want a horse for anyway, Josie-posie?"

"To ride," Josie said, catching up with him.

"Why not a dog, like Miska, or Tiska," Kiff said. "They make great pets." Miska and Tiska were Kiff's twin huskies.

"I don't want a pet," Josie explained. "I want a horse, to be friends with, and teach things, and ride. Horses are partners."

They had reached the blueberry patch where Josie had left her full containers and two empty ones.

"Let's go," Kiff said. "I'll even help you carry these down to the canoe for a small price. Say ten percent of your profits?"

"Forget it, Kokatow," Josie said, slinging the sack of containers over her shoulder. She would take these blueberries over to Kiff's mother and then come back — alone — to look for the horses.

"You get in first," she told Kiff when they had reached the canoe and untied it. "Then I'll hand you the blueberries, and you place them *carefully* in the bottom of the canoe. Got that?" She could just see Kiff tossing the sack to her and missing!

"No faith in me, that's your problem," Kiff muttered as he wobbled his way down the canoe with one hand on each gunnel. "Simple thing, like getting into the canoe..." When he had got himself firmly settled in the bow, he reached back to take the sack Josie was holding out.

"Just hand it to me," he shouted, making a backwards lunge for the bag.

The sudden movement jerked the sack out of Josie's hand and sent the canoe flying. Kiff somersaulted through the air and landed with a mighty splash. The canoe bobbed cheerfully upright again, only half-full of water.

"MY BLUEBERRIES!" Josie screamed. The sack was sinking slowly out of sight. White plastic containers were bobbing to the surface in all directions.

"I'll get them, I'll get them," Kiff sputtered, grabbing for a container that floated out of his reach. He snatched another one and hurled it into the canoe. It burst open, and ripe blueberries showered the seat.

Kiff was a terrible swimmer. His life-jacket kept him afloat, but he did more splashing and thrashing than actual swimming. In a few seconds he managed to spread the berry containers far and wide over the lake.

He snatched at one that was just within reach and the lid flew off. Berries floated around his head like a bright blue collar.

"Don't eat any!" Josie bellowed, so angry she didn't know what she was saying.

"How can I eat?" Kiff spat out a berry. "I'm breathing through my mouth!"

By this time, Josie had managed to get into the canoe. But she was sitting on blueberries, kneeling on blueberries, and feeling them swirl around her bare feet. Kiff lobbed another container that hit Josie's head, covering her in water and blueberries.

"Quit it, Kokatow! Look what you're doing!"

"Okay," Kiff gasped, and started throwing handfuls of floating berries into the canoe. One handful caught Josie in the eye.

She was so angry, she scooped up berries from the bottom of the canoe and fired them back at Kiff.

"HEY! he hollered. "I'm just trying to help!"

Josie grounded the canoe on the rocks. She was blue from head to foot with blueberry juice. "You want to help?" she shouted at him as she gathered up half a dozen stained, wet containers and scrambled up the hill. "Then come and fill these containers again — and this time don't eat them all!"

Kiff had hauled himself up on the ledge and was trying to wring the water out of his shirt again. "I don't know," he complained. "This is the second time you've nearly drowned me in two days!"

Josie stared at him, too astonished to speak. "You hopeless hyper-spaced donut hole!" she finally choked. "I should have *known* better than to bring you!"

Nine

Camp Kokatow

Back at Camp Kokatow, Odie was swinging his feet at the end of the dock. Josie steered the canoe towards him. Her full containers bobbed in the soupy mixture of water and blueberries in the bottom of the boat. She and Kiff had to kneel in this purple soup to paddle, and Kiff had splashed it on his arms, legs and wet clothes.

When Odie saw the inside of the canoe, looking like a blueberry jam jar, and Kiff and Josie splotched purple from head to foot, his hair stood up straighter.

"Did you guys have a food fight?" he asked in awe.

"Yeah," Kiff grinned, "and the food won."

"Help us tie up!" Josie snapped. She wanted to get her containers up to Sheila Kokatow's kitchen and get out of there!

As she marched up the dock she could hear Odie saying, "... something important to tell you, Kiff..." and she caught the words "grandfather" and "horses".

She also heard Kiff's snort of laughter. "Let's go up to my cabin," he said. "I feel a little *blue* in these clothes, if you know what I mean. We can talk there...in *private*."

Kiff sloshed off up the path to the Camp Kokatow cabins. Odie followed hot on his heels. Josie turned towards the camp kitchen and dining hall.

She plopped her six wet, stained containers on the kitchen table. "I'll come back for the money later," Josie panted. "I, uh...have to get home and change."

Sheila Kokatow looked up from rolling pie crust on the long camp table. "More blueberries?" she said gratefully. "You brought these just in time." She stared at Josie's blueberry-stained clothes, and the mangled containers. "It looks like you had a little...trouble, picking them."

"It's a long story," Josie sighed. Wait till Kiff's mom saw *Kiff's* clothes. By now, his entire bedroom would be blue. "I really have to go...."

"See you later. Thanks again!" Sheila sang out as Josie dashed for the door.

She had to find out what those two boys were talking about! It was something to do with her and horses, that much you didn't have to be Einstein to guess.

Kiff's and his parents' sleeping cabins were set off from the guest cabins in a grove of birch trees. Kiff's door was decorated with signs like, "NO HUMAN BEINGS OR JOSIE MOON ALLOWED." He'd put that one up after she'd told on him for shaking up the guests' pop cans. Josie suspected the cabin was also booby-trapped in case she tried to get in.

As if she would! Normally, Josie stayed as far away from Kiff *and* his cabin as she could. But she knew a few things about it, such as Kiff's secret exit in the floor.

She wiggled under the cabin and pushed up the trap door Kiff had sawed through the floor boards.

Kiff's dad would *kill* him if he found out about this! Josie thought as she wedged the trap door open with a stick so she could hear what was going on in-side.

It was mostly giggling.

"Old Moonface was sure she saw a horse, I tell you," she heard Kiff say.

Odie laughed. "You're kidding. Boy, is she strange!"

"I'll get you, Odie Pedersen," Josie vowed under her breath. She was sort of disappointed that Odie would laugh at

her. But when he was with Kiff, Odie
acted just like him.

"Yeah, she's right off her nut this
time," Kiff said gleefully. "Maybe we can
have some fun...."

Josie lay without breathing.

"What did you have in mind?" Odie asked.

"Can you make horse noises?"

"NEIGH-EH-EH." Odie's ringing whinny echoed through the floor boards.

"Hey, that's good, Odie. That's great. And I can make some stomping noises like this." Kiff stamped on the floor. Josie clapped her hands over her ears. What were they planning?

"There's just one problem, Kiff," Odie said. "We don't look like horses."

"She's not going to *see* us. That's the whole point. We get her over by the radar tower. Then we hide, and—"

"I get it!" Odie cried. "We'll make horse noises in the bush. Josie will come after them, and we'll lead her on. Boy, I can't wait to see her face."

"It's diabolical," Kiff laughed. "She's so horse crazy, she's seeing horses behind every bush anyway."

"Poor old Josie Moon," Odie giggled. "We'll lead her on a wild goose chase. Or should I say a wild *horse* chase!"

"And *then*," Kiff was gasping with laughter, "after we've led her up cliffs and through swamps following horse noises, we'll switch to baboon noises, like this: ANH-A-ANH-A-ANH!" Kiff made a high monkey squeal. "And then maybe some pig noises: SNORT-GRUNT-OINK!"

"And how about a cow: MOO-OO-OO!" Odie chuckled.

"She won't know if she's coming or going...."

"And then we'll jump out—" Odie shouted.

"Or come around behind her like we just happened to be there by accident, and ask her what's she's doing!" Kiff laughed.

Josie could hear them rolling around on the floor, laughing hysterically. She carefully lowered the trap door, just as she heard Kiff say, "Let's go down and raid the kitchen. All this laughing has made me hungry."

"Okay by me," Odie agreed. "Think we can lift some of those blueberries Josie brought?"

You wouldn't DARE! Josie wanted to shout. There's just enough for pies!

"Sure," Kiff said. "My mom will never notice a container or two gone."

Lazy slugs! Josie thought. Go pick your own blueberries! As soon as she heard the cabin door slam, Josie wiggled out from under the cabin and hurried back down the hill to her canoe.

Josie had a plan of her own to get even with Kiff, and Odie too! But first she had a lot to do. And she needed to be sure she had seen those horses! It could have been sunstroke, she thought. I can't be positive until I see them again!

On the way down the hill she had the pleasure of hearing Sheila Kokatow shouting at Kiff and Odie to get out of her blueberries and out of her kitchen. Good, Josie thought, I hope she sends them to scrub the outhouse seats. No punishment is bad enough for those two!

She slipped into the canoe and nosed it out into the lake. If she paddled close to shore, Kiff and Odie could not see her from any point on Camp Kokatow's shoreline.

Ten

Josie Sets A Trap

At home, Josie found a note from her mother tacked to the bulletin board:

Dear Josie,
The fire is worse — had to go in to work. Will be back for supper. Go to Kiff's if you need anything.
Love, Mom.

I'll die before I go to Kiff's for anything! Josie thought angrily. But under her anger there was fear. The forest fire must be very bad, if her mother had gone too.

Besides, Josie wished her parents were home so she could tell them about the horses. At least they wouldn't laugh!

Josie stuffed some salami, two pieces of bread, an apple and six carrots into her knapsack, and hurried back to the canoe.

She left a note tacked to the boathouse:

Kiff, Have gone back to Radar Tower Hill to find horses. Josie.

That ought to bring them! Her plan for revenge was in motion. But before she set her trap for Kiff and Odie, there was something she needed in Pedersen's barn.

She could paddle faster than the boys could row. She'd have time to stop at the farm and still get to Radar Tower Hill before them.

****

Odie's grandfather was in the pump house near the lake when Josie finally found him.

"Got to make sure this old pump is working good," he said, wiping his hands. "We might be wetting down the roof before this day is through. They say the fire looks pretty bad. I've seen some big fires in this country. They can wipe out a whole town in fifteen minutes." He shook his head. "What can I do for you, Miss Josie Moon?"

"What would you need to catch a horse?" Josie blurted.

"What horse?" Mr. Pedersen looked sideways at Josie with his sharp blue eyes.

"Can you keep a secret?" she asked. "Even from Odie," she added quickly.

Olaf Pedersen smiled. "I don't have to keep secrets. Nobody pays me much attention these days. I could say, 'A giant troll is coming to eat you up,' and hardly anyone would listen."

"I know how you feel," Josie laughed. "I think, I mean I'm pretty sure I've seen horses, over behind Radar Tower Hill, and I can't get anyone to believe me."

"Horses! In that valley behind the tower?" Olaf Pedersen's bushy eyebrows shot up. "So you want to catch one, to prove you're not making it all up...."

"Partly," Josie agreed.

"Well, to catch one of those horses, you'd probably need a halter...and a long lead rein," Olaf Pedersen said. "Come with me."

Josie could tell that Mr. Pedersen didn't really believe that she'd seen horses either. He was just being nice about it.

In the tack room, he unhooked a tangle of leather straps from the wall. "This here's the halter," he explained. "This part goes over the ears, and this goes around the muzzle."

"Okay," Josie said.

"You hook the lead rein on here." Olaf showed her the metal ring on the side of the halter, and handed her another long leather strap. "Think you can remember all that?"

"I think so. Thanks, Mr. Pedersen," Josie smiled. "I'll bring it all back safely, don't worry."

"No hurry." The old man waved goodbye. "I hope you find your horse!"

As she paddled away from Pedersen's farm, Josie wondered if Kiff had seen her note, and if he and Odie were already hiding somewhere on Radar Tower Hill, ready with their horse noises and monkey noises. She kept a sharp lookout along the shore for the flash of red on the rowboat's bow.

Kiff and Odie would have hidden Kiff's boat, not tied it up at the docking place along the cliff. So Josie was not surprised she didn't see it as she docked. She scrambled up the hill, keeping a sharp lookout for the boys. When she reached the top, she stopped to look in all directions.

A wind had come up, but it was a hot wind. To the northwest, a thick cloud of smoke was gathering. The forest fire! Josie thought. This morning she had seen just one thin spire of smoke. Now it covered the sun with a thick haze.

The meadow looked empty and peaceful. Josie walked down the path to the big pine tree where she had seen the wasps' nest. It was still there, hanging from a low branch, big as a football. In the shadow of the pine boughs it was hard to see.

Josie didn't get too close. All the kids around Big Pickle Lake had been stung by wasps at some time. They were everywhere. They built nests in stumps and porches. Once there had even been a wasps' nest in one of Camp Kokatow's outhouses. The guest who discovered it never came back!

She backed carefully away from the wasps' nest and followed the path to the bottom of the hill. She had last seen the horses come out of the woods to the right. She'd look in that direction.

But first, Josie needed lunch. She walked over to where the radar station cabin used to be. All that was left was a low wall of rocks that used to be the foundation. She sat on the wall and ate her bread and salami.

When she was done, Josie took the halter and rein out of her pack and straightened them out on the ground. She hoped she could remember how they went on!

Finally she put the carrots and apple in her pockets, slung the empty pack on her back, and picked up the halter. It was time to find out if she'd been dreaming or not!

Josie had just stepped into a grove of young poplars when she caught a glimpse of something brown among the grey-green leaves.

Josie fished a carrot out of her pocket and stood perfectly still, holding it in her outstretched hand. She heard a confused chorus of snorts and whinnies and saw flashes of brown and grey and white wheeling through the leaf patterns of sun and shade.

The horses were leaving!

Eleven

Skydive!

Josie stood still, hand outstretched. She could hear the thudding of feet growing fainter in the distance. What idiots Kiff and Odie were to think they could imitate horse noises! Once you heard the real thing you could never forget the sound.

Suddenly, Josie heard a closer noise.

"Skydive!" she breathed, as the grey colt stepped out of the trees. The young horse was more curious than the adult horses. He hadn't run away.

"Here, boy," Josie called gently. "I've got something good for you. Better than grass. See?" She turned very slowly in the colt's direction.

The colt took a step forward. Josie thought her heart would stop, he was so perfect. Of course he wasn't a huge black stallion, and his mane and tail were all matted with burrs but he was here! He was almost within reach.

"Come on, boy," she said again. Skydive looked more shy than afraid. He was definitely interested in the carrot. His nostrils quivered as he took another step forward.

"I wish I had some sugar lumps for you." Josie kept talking in a low, gentle way. "I saw in *The Black Stallion* how the boy made friends with a horse using a big lump of white sugar. But my mom and dad don't believe in white sugar. And the only time I've ever even seen sugar lumps was at the hotel in Timmins. I'll get you some the next time I'm there. In the meantime, how about this carrot?"

The colt was so close that Josie could smell him — a sharp, sweet smell. She didn't dare move in case she startled him. Her arm was beginning to get stiff.

She didn't have much longer to wait. Skydive took one more step and stretched out his neck. His lips wrinkled back and Josie saw his strong teeth. She held her hand flat, while the colt snatched the carrot in one bite, barely touching her hand. All she felt was a sort of wet tickle.

Crunch, crunch. Skydive swung his head as if he were nodding. *Yes, that was quite delicious. Got any more?*

"I've got something better," Josie said. "I've got a whole, green, juicy apple. They're my favourites. I think you'll like them too." She reached slowly into her pocket for the apple and then held it out to Skydive.

He was faster this time. Josie was sure apples smelled at least twice as delicious as carrots. And this time, as he munched, she reached up to pat his neck.

The colt didn't seem to mind. He came closer and sniffed at Josie's pocket, while her hand stroked his silky nose. "It's the only part of you that *is* silky," she laughed. "You sure are a mess, Skydive. Doesn't anyone ever brush you?"

For the second time, Josie wondered who *did* look after the colt. Who owned him, and the other horses?

"I suppose it will be easy enough to find out where you belong," Josie said. "But I don't want to. Right now I want to pretend you're mine."

As she gave Skydive the last carrot she took the halter off her right arm and held it up for him to sniff.

He seemed to know right away the leather was not to eat. He stamped and shook his head as if to say, "Keep that thing away from me!"

"I just want to try it on you," Josie said, wishing she knew what she was doing. "This part goes over your ears and ..."

Skydive was not standing still for this! He snorted and tossed his head again. A sudden high *neigh-eh-eh* from the trees made his ears go flat and his head jerk up. Josie saw fear and confusion in his eyes.

"Steady," Josie said, reaching for his muzzle. She let the halter slide to the ground. "It's just a couple of boys I know, trying to play a dumb joke."

But the colt backed away from Josie's hand, stamping and snorting. Then, with a movement as quick and smooth as water flowing from a glass, he turned and was gone.

Josie was furious! She'd had him so close. He was starting to trust her. And then those two dirtballs...!

Josie knew she had to get Kiff and Odie out of the valley before they frightened the horses so badly that she'd never see them again. It was time to swing into action with her plan!

She stuffed the halter into her knapsack and started back the way she had

come. The boys thought they were leading her? Well, *she* would lead *them*.

The strange high whinny came again.

Josie stopped to listen. The boys
seemed to be somewhere near the bottom of the path. Good! That's just where
she wanted them.

"Here, horsie, horsie," she called — as
if that were any way to get a horse to
come! But it would make Odie and Kiff
think she was fooled by their fake horse
noises.

Josie walked straight towards the
boys. "Nice horsie, good horsie. Now
don't you climb that hill, horsie," she
called.

From a thick stand of fir near the path
came a third whinny, then a softer *nicker-
nicker*.

Good boys! Josie laughed to herself.
Just keep backing up.

Neigh-eh-eh-eh! came Odie's fake whinny. It was a little breathless because Odie
was climbing the steepest part of the hill.

Josie climbed fast, not giving the boys time to change direction. "Here, horsie," she called. "I've got a nice surprise for you, horsie."

They were almost at the big pine tree. The surprise was just above them. With any luck, thought Josie, Kiff and Odie would back right into it.

The wasps were meaner than bees. They could sting and sting again. And they hated to be disturbed.

Just a little higher...

Nicker (pant) *nicker* (pant) *nicker*. It sounded pretty ridiculous to hear a horse pant! Josie waited, hands on hips, for the satisfying scream. When a wasp stung you, everyone screamed. Josie could remember the last sting she had, under her right thumb nail. She hadn't stopped hopping and screaming for fifteen minutes. She could feel the pain right now....

It was Josie that screamed. "STOP! Odie, Kiff, watch out! You're walking into a wasps'nest!" Odie and Kiff were

right under the big pine tree. She heard
scuffling and rustling, then silence.

Twelve

Smoke on Stag Island

When she reached the boys they were standing perfectly still under the pine tree, stunned into silence.

"Holy cow," Kiff whispered at last. "We almost backed right into it. That's a killer nest."

"How did you know we were going to hit the wasps' nest?" Odie asked.

"Because I was herding you towards it. It's easy to herd horses, you know," she grinned.

"You wouldn't!" Kiff stared angrily at her.

"Well, I didn't," Josie said. "But you would have deserved it."

"Look at that thing," Odie breathed, walking around the nest at a safe distance. "It's the biggest nest I've ever seen. There must be hundreds of wasps in there — maybe thousands."

"Maybe we should get a little farther away from it," Kiff muttered.

"Okay," Odie agreed. "But I'm coming back in the fall when it's empty. It would look neat in my room."

"I think Josie should keep it," Kiff said, his eyes twinkling wickedly. "Just to remind her she's getting soft in her old age."

"*Kiff Kokatow!*" Josie roared. "If I had a smaller wasps' nest I'd stuff it down your throat!"

"Temper, temper…" Kiff teased. "Were you over here to look for your horses again, Moonbrain?"

"No, I'm here to pick blueberries," Josie said angrily. It was no use trying to tell them about Skydive, now that they'd scared him away! "I have to get going."

"What you got in the knapsack?" Odie asked as they climbed over the crest of the hill. "Something to eat?"

"None of your business," Josie said. If they saw the halter they'd *really* laugh.

"I'll bet it's full of blueberries, isn't it?" Kiff said, slapping the knapsack on Josie's back. "Hey, no it isn't. It's something hard...and lumpy. What have we here?"

Josie hadn't had time to buckle the flap after she'd stuffed in the halter. As she whirled away from Kiff the whole tangle of leather plopped out on the ground.

"It looks like...like our horse harness," Odie said, surprised.

"How interesting," Kiff nodded, dancing away from Josie's swinging fists.

Josie was mad enough now to tie both the boys up in the tack and march them back to the wasps' nest. Stinging was too good for them. Kiff was right, she was getting soft!

"*Neigh-eh-eh!*" Kiff laughed, bouncing away. "You won't catch us, Ms. Horse-Crazy Moon."

He and Odie took off down the cliff, heading for their boat. "Better see a brain surgeon," Kiff shouted back. "Your condition is getting serious, Moonbrain."

Josie shrugged off her pack and stuffed in the tack. "I'll get even!" she repeated over and over. "Somehow, I'll get even."

She waited at the top of the hill until she saw the Camp Kokatow rowboat pulling away. Then she climbed down, dumped her knapsack in the canoe, and added a rock for weight.

The wind was blowing harder now. Waves were sloshing against the rock ledge, and paddling would be hard without Kiff in the bow. Josie knew the wind would try to blow her straight down the lake, away from Big Pickle Island. She would have to fight it all the way.

She untied the canoe and lifted it into the water. Then she stepped carefully into the centre and shoved off with a paddle. Right away the wind grabbed her bow and swung it down the lake.

Josie crouched low and dug her paddle hard into the water. She wished she were heavier or had stronger arms.

Half an hour later she knew the wind was beating her. Her arms felt like overcooked macaroni. She let the canoe be blown downwind for a few seconds, to rest and think things out.

The sun beat down through a wicked, pinkish-grey haze. A thin film of smoke had spread across the sky, like grease smeared on a clean window.

Just a little to the south lay Stag Island. As Josie gazed at it she thought she saw a thin trickle of smoke rising from the point at the near end of the island.

There was a fireplace for campers on the point, but during a forest fire alert no one was allowed to light a fire outdoors. Josie thought she could make it to the point on Stag Island. While she was waiting for the wind to die she would check out that smoke!

But the wind blew stronger. Harder waves slapped against the side of the canoe. Every stroke forward that Josie gained, the strong gusts blew her back two. The light canoe was like a wood chip scudding across the lake.

"Hey, Josie, that's not the way ho-o-me!" she heard over the water.

"No!" Josie groaned. "Not Kokatow! Not now!" She couldn't break her concentration to look back over her shoulder, but she didn't really need to look. It would be Kiff and Odie plunking along in their old Camp Kokatow rowboat. It was much steadier in the wind than her canoe.

"Slo-o-w down, and we'll give you a t-o-w!" Kiff bellowed.

Josie heard only *slow* and *tow* shouted over the wind. She dug her paddle in hard and twisted it sharply. The bow of the canoe whipped around. Now she was being blown backwards up the lake.

"Well, come on!" she shouted to the rowboat. "I can't hold it like this all day." Josie couldn't let the wind catch the canoe broadside, or it would flip. "Come on! My arms are falling off!" It would have been better to try to make Stag Island on her own. Why did she ever, *ever* listen to Kiff?

Kiff was dangling over the bow of his boat, trying to throw her a rope. Odie, of course, was doing all the work. "Just put your back into it, Odie-boy," Kiff hollered. "We'll have this helpless vessel rescued with just a few mighty strokes of your oars!"

Odie gave one mighty stroke — and Kiff toppled headfirst into the water. This time he barely made a splash! He bobbed up in his life-jacket and made a grab for the side of the canoe.

"Oh, no you don't," Josie yelled. "You're going to tip me!" It was too late. The canoe flipped, and Josie was smacked in the face by an oncoming wave. She grabbed for her knapsack with the precious halter just before it sank out of sight.

"Kokatow!" she yelled, "GET THE CANOE!" The green canoe was blowing away like a leaf in the wind. Kiff clutched for its dragging rope and held on tight.

By this time, Odie had managed to steer the rowboat close enough so that Josie could grab one side and Kiff the other. They glared at each other across the boat.

"We can't both climb in at the same time!" Josie spat lake water. "You first — before you drown."

"Who's drowning?" Kiff grunted, as he threw his thin leg over the side. "You're the one that had to be rescued."

"*Rescued!*" Josie spluttered. "You call this being *rescued!*"

"Oh, don't be such a prunehead." Kiff handed the canoe rope to her. "We were almost across the lake when Odie spotted you. He figured that since you saved us from the wasps, we should save you from being blown away."

"Thanks, Odie," Josie sighed. She tied the canoe to the back of Kiff's rowboat and dumped her sodden knapsack in the bottom.

Odie looked embarrassed. "It seemed like you were in a bit of trouble."

"Nothing I couldn't handle." Josie looked pointedly at Kiff. "I was heading for Stag Island. I thought I saw some smoke on the point."

Odie nodded and set off for Stag Island with a steady stroke. The fireplace on the point was just a ring of stones. Every year campers added a few more rocks or cleared the brush around it so it was safe to light a campfire. But Josie, Kiff and Odie knew that no fire was safe now — not with a big forest fire burning and the sky hung heavy with smoke.

They dragged the rowboat up on the flat rocks at the end of the point. It looked as though fishermen had been using the fireplace. The coals were still smoldering under the remains of a roasted pike. There was crumpled tinfoil and the blackened shell of a can.

"Garbage!" Kiff kicked at the can with disgust. Anyone could camp on Stag Island — it was Crown Land. But most people were careful not to leave garbage behind. "These people are grubs!"

Odie got a can from the boat and dumped water on the smoking coals and the rocks of the fireplace. "They must have just left..." he muttered.

Just then they heard shouting and laughing in the distance.

"They're still here!" Kiff stood up. "Let's make a citizen's arrest!"

"Let's see how big they are first," Odie said.

Josie, Kiff and Odie slipped through the woods, making no sound on the thick carpet of pine needles.

There were three men. They were fishing from the shore of a small bay, and had just pulled in another good-sized pike. All three were wearing light brown pants, red plaid jackets and floppy hats. They were drinking out of aluminum cans.

"Too bad we left the guns in the boat," one man said. "Look at the teeth on this feller!"

"Hunters!" Josie hissed.

"I don't know, Alf. I wouldn't like to see what the old thirty-thirty bear rifle would do to that fish!" laughed another man. "Why don't we just bash him on the head and be done with it?"

"Bear hunters!" Josie stiffened. She hated the hunters who came north to shoot bears for sport. "Are they staying at your camp?" she shot at Kiff.

"Never saw them before in my life," Kiff promised. "Never want to see them again." He was still mad about the garbage.

"They could be staying in a camper down at the landing," Odie said. "What have you got against bear hunters, Josie?"

"They don't hunt fair. They bait traps with food, and sometimes they even tie a live pig to a tree to get the bears to come."

"And they don't want the meat," Kiff added. "They just want a bearskin for the rec room. With its mouth open, like this..." Kiff made a dead-bear-rug-on-the-floor face.

Odie smothered a laugh, but Josie was serious. "My dad says that to the Cree people, the bear is a really important animal," she said. "When a hunter killed a bear, he thanked the bear's spirit for giving him meat and fur. And then he buried the heart to show respect for the bear. These guys just tie a dead bear to the top of their car and roar through town like they've done something big."

"We fish for trophies," Odie said. "You've got a big stuffed pike hanging over your bed. I don't see the difference."

"I guess you're right." Josie couldn't argue. "But it feels different, somehow."

"The difference is," said Kiff, "those guys are big and fat and ugly, and you're short and skinny and ugly."

Josie ignored him. "I wonder where their boat is?" she said. "I'd like to get a look at it."

They found the boat easily. It was tied in a shallow bay on the other side of the island — a large, fancy aluminum fishing boat, with a steering wheel and a sixty horsepower motor.

"There's horses for you, Josie!" Kiff said in admiration.

"From down south." Odie pointed to the numbers stencilled on the bow.

"Okay," Josie said. "I've seen it. Are you guys going to give me a tow home?"

Thirteen

The Fire Closes In

It was a tough row back to Little Pickle Island against the wind.

They all took turns rowing. Kiff and Josie's clothes dried in the hot wind and sun before they reached home. The sun was a hot blob swimming in a rosy haze. It looked like a sunset, but it was only mid-afternoon.

The *Green Hornet* was bobbing at the dock like a cork in a washing machine. "My parents are home," Josie cried. "They'll have news about the fire!"

The news was serious. "The fire has reached the old Timmins road," Bill

Moon told them. "They're thinking of evacuating the town in case the fire swings in that direction."

"I'd better get home," Odie said quietly. He swept his hand over his sticking-up hair. Kiff and Josie glanced at each other. If the fire reached the town it would destroy Pedersen's farm on the way.

"We'll run you over in the *Hornet*," Bill Moon said.

"How far away is the fire?" Josie asked, thinking of her horses. Their valley was also directly in the path of the fire.

"It's still about fifty kilometres away," her dad said. "But the wind is spreading it faster than we can put it out. It started up near Ramore. We never thought it would get this far."

Josie felt a hot flash of fear. Ramore! That's where the wild horses were from. Maybe her horses had moved south and east because of the fire! If they were wild, no one would come to get them.

No one even knew where they were except her.

"But we're not in danger on the islands," Josie's dad told Kiff. "Your camp will be okay."

But what about the wild horses? Josie wanted to shout. *They won't be okay!*

"How did the fire start?" Kiff asked. The red cloud to the west seemed to be growing nearer every second.

"In a barn on an old homestead south of Ramore," Josie's dad said. "We're looking for three bear hunters seen up that way."

"BEAR HUNTERS!" Josie, Kiff and Odie shouted.

"We...we just saw them..." Kiff stammered.

"On Stag Island!" Josie blurted.

"They lit a fire there too," finished Odie.

"Hop in the boat," Josie's father looked grim. "Show me where you saw them."

The *Hornet* flew away from the dock, bucking the waves like a rodeo horse. Josie stole a glance at Kiff. He didn't seem to care about driving the *Hornet*, as long as they could catch the bear hunters!

But when they docked at Stag Island, the bear hunters had gone. "They might be on the mainland," Josie said. "Odie thought they might be camping at the landing."

What was a half-hour row or a twenty-minute canoe paddle was just a couple of minutes in the *Green Hornet*. In no time they had left Odie at his farm and were speeding towards the town of Big Pickle Lake.

The landing was crowded with people, cars and trucks. Everyone in Big Pickle Lake was preparing to evacuate.

"Odie thought the boat was from down south," Josie said as they tied the *Green Hornet* to the dock.

"That'll help," Bill Moon said. "I'd sure like to catch those characters!

Spread out, you two, and see if you can spot that registration number."

Kiff and Josie searched up and down the rows of cars and boat trailers, but found nothing. By the time they got back to Josie's dad, he was talking to a wildlife officer in a green truck.

"It looks like I might be busy here all night," he told Josie. "Your mother too. They'll need every hand if we evacuate the town."

But what about my horses? Josie wanted to shout. She'd been counting on her father's help. If the horses were the wild horses of Ramore, then they were his responsibility. He was the wild animal specialist.

"I'll drop you two at Kiff's camp." Her father was striding back to the dock. "You'll be safe with the Kokatows."

"But Dad! What about my canoe…and pajamas and stuff?" Josie pulled at his arm. Without her canoe, she would be helpless to rescue Skydive and the other horses.

"Kiff can lend you some clothes for tonight. This is an emergency, kid."

"I know, Dad, but..." Josie hurried after him. "Please, could we just go home? I'll be all right by myself."

"We'll feel better if we know you're with Chris and Sheila."

"Couldn't I stay at Odie's instead?" Josie begged. From Pedersen's farm she could hike along the shore to the horses. Odie's grandfather might even help her....

"Josie Moon!" Her father stopped in mid-stride. "Odie's family will have enough to do trying to save their farm. I've had it up to here with you and Kiff fighting. It's childish, it's stupid, and it's got to stop! We need you to be grown-up today!"

"Yeah," Kiff muttered. "Grow up a little, J.M. I'll be happy to lend you my teddy bear. Even though you'd rather stay at Odie's."

Josie was surprised that underneath his teasing, Kiff looked almost as if she'd hurt his feelings. She jumped in the *Green Hornet*, rocking it from side to side.

"But dad, I have to talk to you," Josie tried again. "It's about the horses that I..."

"*Horses!*" Bill Moon shouted as he pushed the throttle of the Hornet wide open. "I can't think about horses now! Where's your sense, Josephine?"

When her father spoke in that tone of voice and called her Josephine, there was no use saying any more. She would just have to figure out how to rescue the horses herself!

Fourteen

Kiff Gets Involved

"Pray for rain!" Sheila Kokatow said as they sat around the camp kitchen before bed that night. "A good long soaking is what we need."

But the next morning the sun rose hot and red. When Josie stepped out of her cabin she could smell the smoke. The air felt thick to breathe.

Josie ran down to the Camp Kokatow dock. Across the lake, the sky was an angry scarlet. Josie thought of her horses, trapped in their narrow valley. I've got to get them out of there! she thought. NOW!

Josie marched up the hill to Kiff's cabin and pounded on the door. She could hear Kiff singing at the top of his lungs inside:

> I'm a little acorn brown,
> Lying on the cold, cold ground,
> Everybody steps on me,
> That is why I'm cracked, you see.
> I'm a nut, I'm a nut, I'm a nut...

You certainly are, Josie thought. She banged on the door again, so hard it shook the panels.

The singing stopped. "Who is it?"

"It's Josie. Kiff, I want to talk to you. Can I come in?"

There were scuttling noises from inside. Kiff was probably rigging the booby traps he had set for her. Josie went around to the back of the cabin and wiggled underneath. She punched up hard on the secret trap door and erupted into the centre of Kiff's room.

He whirled around as if he'd been shot.

The bucket of water he had been precariously balancing over the door slipped and dumped, drenching him from head to toe. Then he tripped over the wire he had stretched across the door-way and landed at her feet.

"*Moonbrain!*" he yelled. "What are you doing in *my room*? How did you know about my secret entrance?"

"I've known about it forever," Josie sneered. "Remember yesterday, when you and Odie were plotting how to sound like horses...Oh!"

Suddenly, Josie was furious. Skydive and the other horses could be burning to death! "I came up here to ask you to help me!" she shouted at him. "But you're so involved in your stupid baby games you're as much use as a wet noodle!"

She brushed past him angrily and burst out the door. There was only one thing to do. She would have to hike across the island, swim to her own is-land, and get her canoe. Grown-ups and

Kiff Kokatow! Josie thought furiously. They never believe you and won't help!

Her anger took her tearing up the hill behind Camp Kokatow. When she got to the top of the island, she stopped for a glance towards the fire. The clouds of black smoke were closer and heavier behind Radar Tower Hill. There wasn't much time.

Josie ran and slid and stumbled down the other side of the island. When she got to the lake she ripped off her shoes, socks and jeans. Little Pickle Island was about 500 metres away. She was forbidden to swim long distances alone, but this was no time for rules. Her canoe was on Little Pickle Island, so that's where she was going!

"Hey Josie, going swimming?" Josie heard behind her.

Josie held her nose and jumped. The water closed over her head. She went down till her toes touched bottom, and came up, gasping. The water was cold.

"Where are you going?" Kiff asked.

"Forget it…" Josie shouted back.

"All right. Don't tell. I'll just take your shoes and pants back to the camp for you." Kiff picked up her clothes and started up the hill.

"Kiff, don't!" Josie tried to yell and tread water at the same time. "I need my shoes. I'm going to get the canoe. Wait there till I paddle back. Okay?"

"If you needed a boat ride, all you had to do was ask…." Kiff shouted in his most maddening voice.

But it was too hard to argue and swim. Josie hoped he wouldn't hide her clothes or do something else stupid. She would need them on Radar Tower Hill.

Josie reached the island and climbed ashore, panting. She had swum farther, but not that fast! She dashed for the house to get her knapsack, a bag of apples and some dry clothes, and raced back to the dock. She loaded the canoe and paddled back to Kiff.

"Are you practicing for the Iron Man Race?" he grinned as he caught the nose of the canoe. "I see you have some food," he went on, holding Josie's shoes out of her reach. "Apples and carrots...that's a weird lunch. I didn't know you were a vegetarian."

"Kiff, for once in your life be useful!" Josie cried. "I need you to help me."

"Help you what?" Josie thought she could see a glimmer of real thought behind Kiff's laughing eyes. She would try one more time.

"I need two people, probably two boats. If I can't catch the horses, I'll have to herd them. There's not much time."

"Moonbeam, you're babbling." Kiff said. "Slow down and tell me in English."

"THE HORSES!" Josie shouted.

Kiff shook his head. "You disappoint me, Josie Moon," he said. "I thought for a minute you were talking about something real."

"I am. They are. Three adult horses and a colt. I think they are the wild horses of Ramore. They got driven down here by the fire. And now they might die unless I help them!"

"You're serious."

"Of course I'm serious. Let go of the canoe. If you want to help, meet me over at the radar tower."

Kiff gave the canoe's nose a shove out into the lake. "And bring some sugar cubes if your parents have any..." Josie shouted.

"This better not be a joke!" Kiff shouted back. He was already running.

Fifteen

The Trap is Sprung

Josie saw something glinting against the rocks as she approached Radar Tower Hill.

She swung the nose of her canoe into the docking place. When she climbed out and pulled the boat up out of the water, she scrambled along the shore to get a better look at the shiny thing she had seen from the water.

It was the bear hunters' boat.

Josie recognized the big motor and the steering wheel, and the plaid jacket one of the men had worn. There were empty bullet boxes in the bottom of the boat, and canvas gun cases.

Josie felt fear trickle up and down her back. What were the bear hunters doing here? She scanned the hillside above for a glimpse of the three men, but everything was still and quiet. She looked impatiently across the lake to where Kiff's rowboat was slowly inching closer.

"Hurry!" she shouted when he was within earshot. "The bear hunters are here!"

"My dad's gone to fight the fire," Kiff yelled back. "They're trying to make a firebreak around the town. Everybody's gone to help."

Josie danced impatiently on the rocks until the bow of Kiff's wood boat thumped against the rocks. She caught the rope that was tied to the front and looped it around a tree. "Hurry!" she told Kiff again. "They've taken their guns."

Kiff whistled when he saw the empty shell cases in the bottom of the hunters' boat. "Those guys aren't out for chipmunks," he said. "A thirty-thirty is for big game."

"Like horses!" Josie said. "Let's go. They must have gone over the hill to the valley."

They climbed the cliff at top speed. "Did you bring some sugar?" Josie panted.

"Yeah, I found an old box," Kiff panted back. "Mom uses those little paper packages of sugar in the dining hall now, but we used to use lumps."

"I don't think sugar goes bad," Josie said as they passed the ledge where they'd picked berries. The blueberries still lay in a thick carpet, but the rest of the world seemed to have changed since Kiff sat there yesterday, stuffing ripe berries into his mouth. Josie felt a million years older.

"Moonbeam," said Kiff, "tell me something. Are there really horses?"

Josie stopped climbing and stared at him. "Do you still think I'm making it up?" she asked. "Because if you do, give me your sugar cubes and go home!"

"No, I guess not." Kiff shook his head. "Do you really think the sugar will make them come to you?"

"Skydive was eating out of my hand," Josie said. "I might have got the halter on him if you and Odie hadn't ruined everything. I don't know if the others will come. They're pretty wild."

"How many others did you say there were?"

"Three. I hope we can find them," Josie said anxiously. "The fire looks close!" The wall of black smoke loomed much closer from the top of the hill. It seemed to be just over the next ridge.

They started down the valley path.

"No sign of the hunters..." Kiff said.

At that exact instant, a deafening *crack* split the air. Then a sickening thud, so close it made them jump, and then the whine of a thousand angry wasps.

"Get down!" Kiff flattened himself

against the ground. "They hit the pine tree."

But Josie was already running, zig-zagging down the hill, heedless of bullets, or wasps, or trees in her way. A second shot rang through the valley. She felt the pain of it in her ears, behind her eyes. They were shooting at her horses!

Another shot, and then another split the hot summer air. Kiff felt terror claw at his insides as he stumbled to his feet after Josie.

He caught up with her at the cabin site, just as the three bear hunters came out of the woods, laughing and shouting. Their voices sounded loud and harsh in the ringing silence that followed the gunshots.

"That sure made 'em take off!" laughed one man.

"That big fellow can really move...." Another hunter shook his head.

They stopped talking when they saw Kiff and Josie, standing very still in the

sunny clearing. Josie felt so angry that
her voice and body seemed far away.

But Kiff cleared his throat and
stepped forward. "I hope you haven't
been shooting at our livestock," he said.

"Livestock? You mean those horses?"
the first man said.

Kiff shot a look at Josie. The look said,
"I believe you" and "I'm sorry" all at
once.

"Those horses belong to us," Kiff said
sternly. "We're pasturing them here for
the summer."

"Well, we didn't hit none of them," the hunter said. "We thought they was a bear."

"Oh," Kiff said. "Is that what you're hunting?"

"Yup," the second hunter joined in. "Always wanted one of them bear-skin rugs for the den."

"They're great, aren't they?" Kiff nodded.

Kiff could talk like that to grown-ups, Josie thought. The way he talked to the fishermen over at his camp.

"Funny you should mention bears," Kiff went on, sounding very excited. "My friend and I just dodged a she bear and her cubs on top of the hill." He pointed up at the radar tower. "Didn't we, Josephine?"

What was Kiff talking about? What bears?

"She's still a little stunned," Kiff shook his head and grinned. "You see, Josephine and the bear reached for the same blueberry. At the same moment."

"Bears? Up there on the hill?" The hunters looked excited. Their eyes got narrow, and their lips got tight.

"Yep. Those bears scooted right down under that big pine tree." Kiff pointed. "I wouldn't be surprised if they have a den, right around there someplace. Right, Josephine?"

"Could you show us?" the third hunter blurted.

"We could point you in the right direction," Kiff said doubtfully. "We wouldn't want to get too close. It might be dangerous. *Wouldn't it, Josephine?*"

Suddenly Josie understood. The wasp tree! She found her voice.

"Right, Christopher. But we could—" she cleared her throat, "point out the spot."

The bear hunters started up the path in single file.

"Spread out." Kiff pointed up through the brush. "Keep your eyes peeled for tracks...."

He shouted directions as the three hunters worked their way slowly towards the pine tree. "Over that way...a little to the left now...that's it...straight ahead...right under the branches..."

Josie held her breath. Just a few steps more. The wasps would be buzzing around furiously after that gunshot....

"EEEYOWWW!! AAAAAAAGH!"

Once you heard someone being stung by wasps you never forgot the sound. Kiff and Josie saw three blurs of red plaid streaking straight up the hill.

"Those wasps came in handy, after all," Kiff laughed. "They probably won't stop running till they get back to Brampton, or wherever they're from."

Josie shook her head. "You made them believe all that stuff about the bears," she said. "If I could tell the truth as well as you tell lies you might have believed me about the horses!"

"Sorry about that," Kiff grinned. "Do you still have that halter?"

Josie patted her knapsack.

"Then let's go find them." Kiff glanced up at the smoke. "We don't have much time."

Sixteen

Wild Horse Ride

"Smell that!" Kiff said as they plunged into the brush at the south end of the clearing. The smoke burned their eyes and the backs of their throats.

"We've got to find the horses," Josie said. "They must be so frightened. The smoke, and the shots...we've got to find them!"

"What'll we do when we find them?"

"I think we should try to get behind them and herd them towards the lake," Josie said. "Just in case we can't catch them."

"Nice plan, Cowboy Jo," Kiff nodded. "What happens when we herd them to the top of Radar Tower Hill? Do they just take a dive off the cliff into the lake?"

"You're right," Josie groaned. She was beginning to think Kiff had been right all along. She was just playing cowgirl. The whole thing was crazy! How could two kids, on foot, herd four wild horses?

"Maybe we should go for help," Kiff suggested.

"Everyone's too busy trying to save the town to worry about horses," Josie shook her head. "We'll have to do it ourselves."

But she was feeling more frightened than she wanted to admit. She sank down on the old foundation wall and buried her head in her arms. What if it was hopeless? What if there was nothing she and Kiff could do?

"I guess you're right," she murmured. "We should get out of here, and try to get some help." She was starting to stand up when she glanced at Kiff.

130

He was standing, frozen as a statue, staring at something just behind her.

"What's wrong?" She suddenly felt a hard nudge under her arm, and then another.

"I think she wants an apple," Kiff managed to say in a whisper, without moving his lips.

Josie slowly turned her head. A huge grey mare was trying to get her nose into Josie's pocket, where she could smell the apples. Her soft, velvety nose was nudging Josie's arm.

"You must be Skydive's mother," Josie said in wonder. She spoke in the same low, soothing voice she had used with Skydive. "And what can I do for you?" She slowly reached into her pocket and got out an apple.

The big grey horse took it off her hand and crunched it in two bites. She tossed her head as if to say, "More, please."

"Oh, but wait till you see what Kiff has in his pockets for you," Josie went on. She hoped Kiff wouldn't blow it all by making some quick, jerky movement or shouting. Kiff's main experience with animals was with husky dogs and fish.

But Kiff slowly reached down into his pocket and pulled out a sugar cube. He held it on his outstretched hand and started to sing in a croaky voice.

There was blood on the saddle...

"Oh, no!" Josie groaned. The mare tossed her head.

But Kiff kept going.

And blood on the ground...

The big horse took a few steps and whinnied. Josie bit her lip. If Kokatow scared her away now, she'd *strangle* him.

But the horse wasn't running away. She edged closer to Kiff, until she could reach out and nab the cube of sugar.

O pity the cowboy, all bloody and red,
And look who's coming for sugar instead!

Josie turned around again. Two more curious noses poked out of the brush. One belonged to a brown mare, smaller than the grey horse. The other belonged to a chestnut stallion, the largest of all. His eyes looked wild and frightened.

"Hello," Josie said softly. "Never mind that horrible noise. It's just Kiff Kokatow singing."

She dug in her pockets for an apple. But the other horses seemed too nervous to come so near. Josie put the apple back and reached for her knapsack. She got out the halter and slowly stood up.

"I'm going to try to put this on your horse," she told Kiff. "She seems the tamest. Maybe we can lead her and the others will follow."

She held the halter up to the grey mare's nose. The mare nickered softly and nodded her head, as if she remembered exactly what the bridle was. Josie slid one part up and over her ears and the other around her muzzle. Then she clipped the lead rein onto the halter.

"It's amazing," she grinned at Kiff. "It's as if she's done this a thousand times before."

"What do you mean?" Kiff snorted. "She just appreciates my great singing." He pointed back at the ridge behind them where the wall of black smoke billowed angrily. "We'd better get out of here, Josie Moon."

"But where is Skydive?" Josie said anxiously. "We can't leave without him."

Suddenly there was a great roar, like the wind rushing through a thousand pines. Josie saw tree after tree on the ridge to the west burst into flame, as if they were wicks on the candles of a giant birthday cake.

"Let's get these guys up to the radar tower, and *fast!*" Kiff shouted. "We'll worry about how to get them down the cliff later."

"But we can't leave without Skydive!" Josie shouted back. "He must be around here somewhere!"

There was another *whoosh* of flame. The fire had jumped the valley on sparks blown by the wind. The radar tower ridge was burning too! The horses whinnied in fear. Josie held tight to the mare's rein and patted her neck.

"Kiff, what now?" she shouted above the roar of the fire.

"We're cut off!" Kiff's face had turned white.

Just then Josie heard a high, urgent whinny. She whirled around, and there was Skydive. He raced from the trees on the south end of the clearing, then wheeled and raced back. The other horses answered his neighing, as if they too were shouting back and forth.

"He wants us to go with him," Josie yelled. "Look!"

"There's no way out to the lake down there," Kiff shouted back. "It's just bush, and the ridge must be burning there too!"

"Skydive must have found some way," Josie called. "Come on, Kiff, we've got to try!" The smoke and flames were closing in on the clearing. The horses whinnied in fear, but seemed glad to follow when they turned and went after Skydive.

"Where's he taking us?" Kiff cried. "I think this is just a dead end, Josie."

But they could not go back. Already the crackling of fire and the great rushing roar when a pine tree burst into flames was fierce behind them. Josie dropped the mare's rein. All of them followed the little colt's dash through the trees.

They seemed to go on forever. Josie could hear Kiff panting behind her and the horses crashing through the brush ahead.

The thick smoke was making it hard to see. Josie almost ran into the wall of a small building before she saw it. There were several small shacks in a cluster, and pieces of rusty equipment.

All at once, Josie realized that Skydive was no longer with them. She heard the rattling of gravel and looked down. The colt was half scrambling, half falling down a steep slope into a deep grey trench. At this end the trench was sloped, but both sides were cut as straight out of the rock as a block of cheese. At the other end of the trench something sparkled through the smoke. Something blue.

"Kiff!" Josie cried. "This must be the top end of the old barite mine. That's the *lake*! Come on!"

They followed the plunging horses down the gravel slope. At the bottom of the trench ran two rails, like a narrow railway line. The mine pit was like a long, narrow notch cut into the side of the cliff.

It was cooler down in the narrow trench, and the air was a little easier to breathe. Above them, the smoke and flames billowed like a fiery roof.

The horses made a last dash through the cloud of smoke at the end of the trench and splashed into the water. Kiff and Josie splashed after them.

The water was warm near the shore, full of ashes and small swimming animals. Josie struck out for deeper, cooler water, and fresher air.

"Wait," Kiff shouted. "Wait! You know I'm a terrible swimmer!"

Josie wanted to laugh hysterically. She knew!

But one glance back convinced her Kiff really was in trouble. His dog-paddling was much worse than usual, and he was gasping for air. Josie treaded water and looked around. The whole shoreline, stretching in both directions, was burning. They would have to swim to Stag Island, almost a kilometre away. Kiff would never make it.

Like Josie, the horses were heading for deeper water. "Let's try to ride on their backs," Josie shouted. She swam over to Skydive.

"Get on the grey horse," she urged Kiff. "And sing! She likes your singing, remember? Hold on around her neck and grip her back with your knees."

"Are you sure?" Kiff yelled. "I've never ridden a horse." He did his crazy dog-paddle over to the grey mare, and sang through gulps of water.

O the Old Grey Mare,
She ain't (gulp) what she used to be,
Ain't what she (gulp) used to be...

"Not that song!" This time, Josie did shout with laughter. But the grey horse didn't seem to mind. She moved smoothly off through the water, with Kiff clinging fiercely to her mane.

Josie threw her leg over Skydive's back. It was a great feeling, being carried through the water on the back of a strongly swimming horse. Skydive turned back once to look at her as if to say, "You? Well, all right, if you insist."

The air got clearer and the water cooler as they swam towards Stag Island. The horses seemed to know by instinct to head for the nearest piece of forest that wasn't burning. Josie could see the heads of the two other horses, surging through the water behind them.

Josie and Kiff slipped from the horses' backs when they were still a few metres from the shore, and swam the rest of the way.

"Well," puffed Kiff, as he staggered up on the shore, "another daring rescue mission completed. I guess we saved your horses, eh, Moonie?"

"They saved us, you mean!" Josie laughed with relief. "I think you'd better take swimming lessons this summer, Kokatow."

Seventeen

A Horse For Josie Moon

"Josie," said Kiff, "do you smell smoke?"

"Very funny," Josie murmured. "The whole forest is burning, and you want to know if I smell smoke?"

They were stretched out on smooth flat rocks on the shore of Stag Island. Their legs and arms ached from the effort of hanging on to the swimming horses. The sky above them was black with smoke and ash, and the wind had turned. Huge dark clouds were moving in from the north. Kiff and Josie hardly noticed the change in the weather, but the chestnut stallion did. He lifted his head to sniff the wind.

The other three horses were grazing quietly near Kiff and Josie, but the stallion stood apart, as if he wasn't sure about these strange creatures yet.

"No," said Kiff, sitting up and sniffing, "I don't mean forest fire kind of smoke. I mean campfire smoke, with coffee brewing, right here on this island."

"But who would be stupid enough to light a campfire when — Oh No!" Josie sat straight up. "Not them!"

"Who *else* would be stupid enough?" Kiff stood up and stretched. "This is where they camped before. Want to take a look?"

They slipped through the trees to the point. There was a small round tent set up behind the campfire. Kiff and Josie could hear muttered curses and groans coming from inside.

"They're probably slathering ointment on their wasp stings," Kiff whispered.

The hunters' big fishing boat was pulled carelessly up at the edge of the point, and a big fire was blazing away in the circle of stones.

"Look at the size of that fire!" Josie said disgustedly. "And nobody's even watching it."

"Keep your voice down," Kiff whispered. "They might not be too happy to see us, after that little accident with the wasps."

Josie was suddenly afraid. "You're right," she said. "They might shoot at the horses again."

"At the horses!" Kiff whispered urgently. "They might shoot at *us!*"

"We could try to stay down at the other end of the island," Josie suggested.

"I'd like to be rescued from this place one of these days," Kiff pointed out. "I'm getting hungry for a marshmallow and banana sandwich. If we want to flag down a boat, we need to be right here on the point."

"You're right," Josie nodded.
"Anyway, we can't just leave this huge fire burning." She found a plastic pail and filled it with lake water. Kiff was peering into the hunters' boat. "What are you doing?" Josie whispered.

Kiff motioned her over. "Look," he whispered. "Their guns are still in the boat. Pretty sloppy hunters. Especially since it's going to rain."

Josie stared at Kiff. "Rain?" she said. "What rain?"

"Look at the sky." Kiff pointed north. "If that isn't a famous Big Pickle Lake thunderstorm rolling in, then I never saw one."

RAIN! Josie wanted to shout, to dance, to hug Kiff Kokatow. It was true; the thunderheads were piling up with amazing speed. What had Kiff's mother said? A good, hard, soaking rain. That's what they needed!

Just then the tent flap burst open. "Who's out there?" came a growly voice. Kiff and Josie turned around to see a fat man on all fours, filling the entrance to the tent.

"Hey, it's you!" the man growled. "What are you doing near our boat? You little...Wait till I get my hands on you!" He was struggling to get out of the tent with his friends pushing and shoving from behind.

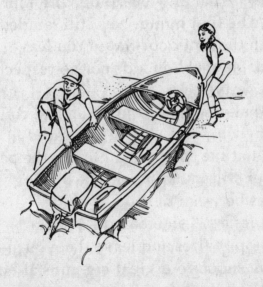

Kiff looked at Josie, and Josie looked at Kiff, and they both looked at the big shiny fishing boat.

"Kiff," Josie said, "You know how you've always wanted to drive a fast boat...?"

"Josie," said Kiff, "I didn't think you'd ever suggest such a thing!" He was already pushing the hunters' boat into the water. "It looks pretty easy to start...."

"Hey! What are you doing with that boat!" The first hunter was still tangled up with the tent door-flap. "You leave that boat alone! You kids got no respect for property...."

At that moment, Josie Moon lost control. She whipped around and raced straight at the astounded hunter, the pail of water still in her hand. The blazing fire was between them.

"*No respect!*" she roared. "*You* start huge sloppy fires and leave them burning! *You* shoot your great big guns at horses, or bears, or anything that moves! *You* probably started a forest fire that has wiped out public property from here to

Ramore! Respect for property? Where's *your* respect?!"

"Josie!" Kiff shouted. "Get in the boat!" The big engine burst into life.

The first hunter had wiggled free and was lurching to his feet. The second was right behind him, and at the sound of the motor, his face grew even uglier than his friend's.

Josie was so mad she could hardly see straight. "All those animals!," she screamed. "And all those trees! We're going to go get the police and — "

"JOSIE! for Pete's sake come on!"

Kiff revved the engine in reverse, but the bow of the hunters' boat was still grounded on the rocks.

All three hunters were now moving quickly toward Josie. Like a small demon of fury, she dashed the pail of water right at their faces. Most of the water sloshed into the fire. A cloud of steam and smoke billowed up. Josie tore towards the boat, gave the bow a mighty shove, and leaped aboard.

The hunters were right behind her, wading into the water. But the rocks were slippery and threw them off balance as they lunged and grabbed for the boat.

"Go Kiff!" Josie shouted. The engine bellowed and the boat surged backwards away from the rocks.

The three hunters roared and cursed and shook their fists. As Kiff and Josie zoomed away, the first huge drops of rain sizzled on the surface of the lake.

"Don't you think they look a bit like bears themselves?" Josie shouted at Kiff.

"Bears are a lot better looking!" Kiff shouted back. "Maybe we should go back and make a citizen's arrest before the rain puts that fire out."

"Maybe we should go for help first," Josie grinned.

****

The next morning, four soft noses poked curiously out of four stalls in Pedersen's barn as Josie came along with a bucket of carrots. Odie's grandfather had supervised getting the horses off Stag Island, once the fire danger was over. The police had rescued the hunters!

Odie was in the stall with the small brown mare, giving her coat a good brush.

"It was great of your grandfather to let us use his barn, till we figure out what to do with the horses," Josie said, stroking Skydive's soft grey nose and offering him a carrot to munch.

"Grandpa likes having the horses around," Odie laughed. "He wants to keep the stallion, if nobody claims him."

Josie offered the stallion a carrot, but he backed away, snorting. "He's going to take a lot of taming," Josie sighed. "Your grandfather thinks he's the only really wild horse. He says the others are used to people. Some hobby farmer must have abandoned them." Josie couldn't imagine how anyone could abandon a horse!

Kiff sauntered into the barn, trying to whistle and eat at the same time. He patted the nose of the big grey mare and dug a sugar cube out of his pocket for her.

"Poor old Skydive," he said. "All he ever gets are carrots."

"Smoky will get fat, eating sugar," Josie said. Kiff had named the mare.

"Speaking of fat," Kiff grinned, "what's the latest on our mighty hunters?"

"A mighty big fine for setting fires when there was a fire ban in effect," Josie said. "And they'll probably be charged with setting the big fire...*and* they're going home with no bear draped over their hood."

"But they'll have some fond memories," Kiff laughed. "Odie, you should have seen them take off with the wasps after them. They looked like they were shot from guns themselves!"

"Are your parents going to let you keep Smoky?" Josie asked, nestling her face against Skydive's nose.

Her mother and father had decided that if it was all right with Olaf Pedersen, she could keep Skydive. Of course there was a long list of other conditions. Josie had to look after Skydive, and work to help pay for his food, and help with the barn chores. A lot of hard work went along with her dream, Josie was discovering. She didn't mind. The work just made it seem more real. Skydive would actually be *her* horse! It seemed too good to be true, but when she stroked his warm, velvety nose, and smelled his warm horse smell, she knew it *was* true.

"Ordinarily," Kiff said, "nothing could be further from my mind than wanting a horse. "But these are not ordinary horses, Josephine. These horses are heroes!"

"Because they saved you, you mean?" Josie laughed.

"Of course," Kiff grinned. "Besides,
I'm obviously a naturally good rider."

"Better at riding than swimming,
that's for sure," Josie teased.

"It could be fun." Kiff pretended to ig-
nore her. "Not as much fun as a fast

boat, but interesting." He patted the nose of the big grey mare.

"A horse that big will eat an awful lot." Josie shook her head. "You'll have to get a job to buy hay, and horseshoes, and a saddle and bridle." She grinned at him. "I suppose you could make money picking blueberries, if you taped your mouth shut."

"Moonbrain, if I didn't know you better, I'd think you were trying to get my goat — I mean my horse!"

Josie just grinned. Sharing a stable with Kiff might be fun!